Published by CreateSpace, a DBA of
On-Demand Publishing, LLC
www.createspace.com

Printed and bounded in the United States of America.

RMJTNB books
ISBN-13: 978-0692093863
ISBN-10: 0692093869

ANXIOUS ADDY CAN'T SLEEP

Written by Monica S. Plack and authored with Bailey E. Plack

Meet Anxious Addy.

Anxious Addy worries about everything...

Anxious Addy worries about going to bed.

... and when to wake up.

Anxious Addy worries about scary noises in the room. Are there people? Monsters? Aliens? Spiders? Animals?

Anxious Addy does not like to be far from Mom and Dad
in the dark.

Anxious Addy is afraid of the dark.

Mom and Dad tuck in Anxious Addy every night...

And every night Anxious Addy creeps into Mom and Dad's bed. Anxious Addy is always nervous and scared.

Anxious Addy is getting older, and Mom and Dad want Addy to sleep in bed VERY soon!

Even Addy's younger sister sleeps in her bed alone.

Everything Addy's parents try doesn't work. Anxious Addy ends up back in Mom and Dad's bed...

So Anxious Addy's Mom and Dad take Addy to the sleep doctor, Dr. Dreams. The doctor and Anxious Addy made a deal to work together on sleeping better through the night and in the right bed.

First, the Dr. Dreams tells Anxious Addy to get 10 hours of sleep to feel the best. That means the new bedtime has to be at 8:00pm.

Next, Dr. Dreams tells Addy to do some fun things before bedtime. She teaches her about imagination vacations, flashlight scavenger hunts, deep breathing, relaxation noises and music.

Dr. Dreams says no TV or electronics in the room at night. This is really sad (and quite scary) but Anxious Addy wants to sleep so Addy agrees to the deal. Instead, Anxious Addy has to do a quiet activity like reading, coloring or playing with toys before bed in the bedroom..

RESPONSIBILITIES CHART

	SUN	MON	TUE	WED	THU	FRI	SAT
No electronics							
Bedtime at 8							
Flashlight scavenger hunt							
Sleeps on sleeping bag							
Follows bedtime routine							

REWARD CHART

Toy	20 points
Book	10 points
Games	15 points
Ice cream	10 points
Bowling	20 points

Next, Dr. Dreams makes a fun chart to help Anxious Addy get reward points for sleeping alone in bed and following the bedtime rules. Addy gets to spend the points earned on fun things like movies, toys, games and activities!

And then Anxious Addy begins the sleep trial... Addy must follow the bedtime routine every night.

Anxious Addy gets 2 bedtime passes to come get hugs from Mom and Dad each night. But then, Addy must go back to bed. Sometimes it works... And sometimes it doesn't...

Now, when Anxious Addy is too nervous to go back to bed, Addy must sleep on a sleeping bag in Mom and Dad's room, not their bed anymore.
Little by little, Mom and Dad will move the sleeping bag closer to Addy's bed each night.

Anxious Addy is earning points every day! Addy is becoming less scared! Addy has even decided the bed is really comfy!

And the sounds are really from things Addy knows and loves...
Not monsters, strangers, aliens, or animals.

Anxious Addy is sleeping
in bed more and more...
Addy even feels better
in the morning now!

Mom and Dad are super proud of Addy! Addy gets to spend the points earned on ice cream, a dinner night with mom, ice skating, movies with dad, a new hamster, a new toy and other fun things!

Soon Addy sleeps in bed every night! And, Addy doesn't have to see Dr. Dreams anymore!

And Anxious Addy isn't Anxious any more! Addy's favorite room is the bedroom with the comfy bed! Every night! And now Anxious Addy feels like Awesome Addy!

This book is dedicated to my precious daughter, who has overcome so much in her young life. Most recently, she has overcome her fear of sleeping that she has had since birth. She helped in the creation of this character and book series in helping others overcome their fears.

I wanted to add a Parent Resource Guide at the end of this book. I am an occupational therapist with a background in many areas, including work with anxiety and have had many hours of continuing education focusing on mental health areas. However, I feel my best experience has been drawn from parenting my own children. I have learned that my husband and I did many things incorrectly when it came to a nighttime routine and rules with both of our children. Unfortunately, possibly like you, it was a little too late to turn back without some help and strategies from an outside source.

First thing, looking back I would have fought through my sleepiness and fought back a little harder and been firmer with my children and the bedtime routine. Like many mothers and fathers around the globe, by the time I finished the day filled with work, followed by baseball games, volleyball, band, dance, grocery shopping, dinner prep and cleanup, I didn't have much energy left for arguing with my overly dramatic daughter about sleeping in her own bed. We began a vicious cycle back when she was old enough to climb out of her bed and come into our room. Although many many many times we would escort her back to bed after our nightly routine, we often would fail after the 4th-- "Im hungry... I have to pee… I'm cold… I'm scared". Eventually she would end up in our bed to fall asleep with mom and dad. My husband would often carry her back to her bed later in the night, but within the next several hours, my daughter would walk or stumble her way back to our bed. Again, after a few trips back to her bed, eventually we caved. This continued on and on until she was ten. We can barely remember a night that we would sleep through the night.

Actually, looking back on social media memories, I would post every few years from the time she was four years old a comment to the fact "I hope my child starts sleeping through the night before she goes to college". College... That seemed like our reality of when we would gain a peaceful night's sleep.

In addition to my 10 year old daughter struggling with nighttime separation anxiety, she also suffered with separation anxiety throughout the day. To add to the mix, she was also diagnosed with generalized anxiety disorder. But worst of all, at such a tender age, she had to learn about what panic attacks are, and how to deal with them.

Only a mother or father of a child with anxiety can understand what it is like not to be able to console your child who is being unreasonable (through no fault of their own), due to the anxiety taking over. To watch your child in a full blown panic attack and thinking they are going to pass out, vomit, collapse, and them feeling like they could possibly die is an awful thing! I am beginning this book series with the issue of sleeping through the night, but there will be other books regarding other issues we have conquered along the way such as going to the doctor, going to the hospital, going to school, sleepovers, etc. I also tried to make the character unisex so boys and girls could both relate to the child in my series.

When our daughter reached ten years old my husband and I had had enough. Although we had seen multiple psychologists and counselors over the years with her, we decided to get a referral to a pulmonologist to evaluate her sleep disturbance. In addition to completing a sleep study, he referred her to a psychologist who specializes in children with sleep disorders. This was an answer to prayers! Little did we know this appointment would change our life and the life of our child who was a slave to her fear and anxiety. Little did we know that all of us would eventually be able to sleep through the night again. And more importantly, we didn't know that with some pretty easy recommendations, we could implement a new routine and finally sleep again!

In ten years, we did not just skip over the nighttime trials of sleeping in her own bed. We tried everything that we could think of: We tried rewards, bribery, anger, light on, light off, salt lamp, sound box, going to bed with the TV on, going to bed with the TV off, no electronics before bed, Melatonin in various doses, diphenhydramine, stuffed animal or comfort item, electric blanket, fans, memory foam overlay to make the bed more comfy than ours and many, many prayers! NOTHING worked long or successfully! Although, some of these things were bits and pieces utilized by the psychologist, we were not putting it all together correctly. Through the insight we were provided, it truly changed our daughter's life.

I would recommend trialing the things recommended in this book, and my prayer would be that it will help your little child. If you continue to struggle, I would highly recommend seeking out a psychologist who has experience with sleep disorders. Ours was provided at the Pulmonology Department at the local Children's Hospital in our area. I am sure many counselors have experience and great insight into these problems as well. We, unfortunately, didn't successfully fix this problem with any previous counselors because often we were focusing on anxiety versus the sleep disturbance.

Before you embark on the process of changing the sleep habits of your child, plan to have a discussion to sit down and establish a "Plan" together. This worked well for us because we went to a psychologist to implement and assign what we were to do. If you are beginning theses methods on your own at home, there needs to be a clear day to "Begin." This will allow a clear boundary for follow through. Using the methods in this book and the Responsibilities Chart, you and your child can work together to create healthy sleeping habits. As a parent, this is the time to tell yourself that you are going to be firm and follow through with the strategies. From what we learned, consistency was the key this time around. Every time my spouse and I let up and allowed my child to fall asleep in my bed, she would revert back to old routines and we would regret it.

The biggest and best intervention that we were provided through our time with the psychologist was a Responsibility Chart that correlated with a Reward Chart. These can be modified and changed throughout the course of progress to address other areas as well, as deemed necessary. With the Responsibility Chart, the child is able to earn points for successfully completing the areas that need addressed. This allows the parents to keep track of the progress as well as points being earned and utilized for rewards. Rewards can be small point values or large point values depending on how often your child needs positive reinforcement. Small items such as going for ice cream could be 10 points that could successfully be earned after 2-3 days. Likewise, items such as a new toy, roller skating, or bowling could be worth higher point values. Cautiousness needs to be taken to not allow points to be saved up too long which loses the positive reinforcement effectiveness of the chart/reward system.

I found that keeping a bag of goodies on hand that allowed her to choose helped me to be able to implement a reward when I didn't have time to take her to the movies, bowling, ice cream etc.
I included "grab bag item" on her chart so we were constantly trying to reward her positive steps forward. A sample has been included that can be used and modified for your own child.
Also included is a sample similar to the one that my daughter started out with for your reference.
Personalization such as pictures or stickers can also be included to help the child with establishing ownership in his/her own recovery. Although I would have never thought about including this, the Psychologist really ask her opinion in placing graphics, colors and the overall design of the chart.
My daughter was excited to have her own personal chart to work on and definitely had ownership with this because of her input.

Responsibility Chart

Place sticker here

Task	Sunday	Monday	Tuesday	Weds	Thursday	Friday	Saturday

Responsibility Chart

Place sticker here

Task	Sunday	Monday	Tuesday	Weds	Thursday	Friday	Saturday
Follow Bedtime Routine							
Electronics Off 1 hr Before bed							
Bedtime Passes							
Flashlight Scavenger Hunt							
Relaxation technique							

Reward Chart

Reward	Points Needed to earn

Nighttime Routine

The first thing we had to establish was a night time routine. A night time routine is essential in preparing the child's mind and body for sleep. Following a routine is key in allowing them to focus on the fact they will be going to bed. Unfortunately, this is not always easy right off the bat because thinking about the item (bedtime) which causes the anxiety, just creates more anxiety. Eventually, we were providing a time limit for our daughter's night time routine where she received a point for completing all her tasks within the established time frame. (Ours was 30 minutes) Without a boundary, her routine could take hours.

It is helpful to make a list with pictures or words based on their age so they can follow the routine with some ownership and confidence of self completion. Children with anxiety like routines. They like to know the expectations and the plan. Most children with anxiety thrive with routines because it provides a sense of normalcy, and they know what is expected and what is coming up next.
Part of the routine is ensuring an appropriate bedtime. Based on my experience with my four children and talking with other parents, this is a recommended bedtime. Talk with your child's doctor regarding specific recommendations for bedtimes for additional questions. Every school has a different start time and end time and every family has a different family dynamic and schedule they must follow. But basically, children need sleep. Plenty of it!

Children need sleep. Children function better with enough sleep. Anxiety decreases with sleep. Their bodies are able to recover and regenerate. Once my child began getting a full night sleep, she began to love to sleep. She actually stated, "I never knew I could feel this good in the morning. I feel so refreshed." I really wasn't as concerned about the lack of sleep because from the time she was born she always woke up at 7 am like clockwork no matter her bedtime. I was clearly wrong in my thinking. She is much calmer, much clearer in her thinking, and she verbalizes her restfulness.

First, I would initiate the bedtime routine as you are reading the rest of the book. This will allow the child to be used to the bedtime routine as you are establishing the new rules and expectations recommended in this book.

Wake up time	6:00am	6:15am	6:30am	6:45am	7:00am	7:15am	7:30am
Age	**Bedtime**						
5	6:45pm	7:00pm	7:15pm	7:30pm	7:45pm	8:00pm	8:15pm
6	7:00pm	7:15pm	7:30pm	7:45pm	8:00pm	8:15pm	8:30pm
7	7:15pm	7:30pm	7:45pm	8:00pm	8:15pm	8:30pm	8:45pm
8	7:30pm	7:45pm	8:00pm	8:15pm	8:30pm	8:45pm	9:00pm
9	7:45pm	8:00pm	8:15pm	8:30pm	8:45pm	9:00pm	9:15pm
10	8:00pm	8:15pm	8:30pm	8:45pm	9:00pm	9:15pm	9:30pm
11	8:15pm	8:30pm	8:45pm	9:00pm	9:15pm	9:30pm	9:45pm
12	8:30pm	8:45pm	9:00pm	9:15pm	9:30pm	9:45pm	10:00pm

Relaxation Techniques

One of the techniques that worked well for my daughter and continues to work well is a technique called imagination vacations. This is a relaxation technique that is used as part of her bedtime routine as well as in the middle of the night, if needed, to focus her thoughts on something positive. In this technique, we choose a place we would like to imagine that we are. Some examples we choose is a land of candy, the beach, a cruise ship, an amusement park, or a zoo. We close our eyes and visualize being in the area of choice. We discuss what we see, hear, smell, taste and touch. It's a fun technique to refocus thoughts to something positive and healthy versus focusing on fear, anxiety, the darkness or the separation. This is also used in the middle of the night if scary thoughts have crept in. This shifts focus to something positive and pleasant. This was a simple but fun activity that only lasted several minutes but my daughter enjoyed.

Another technique that can be used during nightmares is making the scary into something comical. An example of this was created by my daughter. She had a nightmare that someone was trying to grab her. When she woke up she envisioned she was just a stuffed animal in a claw machine that got grabbed and then hugged by the child who retrieved the toy. Sometimes she will return to bed and then dream about the positive idea she has just created. This would be the goal of this technique. Most times initially, my daughter needed me to come up with the new comical thought because she was in fear/anxiety-mode.

My daughter, probably like many children in this era, had become accustomed to going to bed watching an electronic device. The bright lights on tablets and phones do not allow the body to relax into sleep mode. We had to explain that we would be removing her electronics from her now to better allow her to sleep and replace it with relaxation techniques. This has proved a pretty challenging thing to accomplish with a child who has used a tablet since she was three. Overall, when she realized the benefits of the sleep, she complies with the new set of rules most of the time. Ultimately, children are children, and this is all a process and improvements are made little by little.

Another thing we have used is deep breathing techniques. We were able to find many apps for children's relaxation breathing that we utilized. This teaches children to relax and gain control over their own breathing. This in turn, will allow their body to relax and anxiety to lessen. I placed them on my phone initially so I knew she wasn't having access to the electronics. As my child progressed, she searched for apps she enjoys listening to. There are many options for breathing techniques. There are verbalizations that parents can read to the child, relaxation CD's, interactive apps to play, and videos than can be searched with an easy click of a button. Eventually my child discovered that the main thing she enjoys best is a personalized lullaby with her name that she listens to every night. She has access to this on her tablet when she goes for sleepovers now in order to maintain her routine (although she listens to it on a tablet vs a CD player at a friend's home). My daughter recognizes how her body feels the moment she begins to play her lullaby and her body relaxes.

Flashlight Scavenger Hunts

Another technique that worked extremely well in conquering her fear of the dark was flashlight scavenger hunts. If you asked my daughter early on about her fear of the dark she would deny it. Even as we began these hunts, she could not process her fear of the dark as her fear of darkness. She just knew that being in her room alone evoked a negative, scary anxiety response.

Flashlight scavenger hunts allow them to look for an item while in darkness. These begin with an extremely easy object to find and continue to get harder as the child is more comfortable with the darkness, silence and the small noises that happen in the silence. First, the lights are off and there is an established object that is "hunted" for. They are provided a flashlight to use for assistance. The item "hunted for" can change based on the complexity of how hard it is being hidden. Larger, easier to find prizes can be used as well if this is a particularly anxiety provoking activity for the child. This will allow the child to locate the item easier with less time spent in the room in darkness. (It can also change based on how tired Mom and Dad are at the time they are hiding it. Sometimes I would hide things in the morning that she would not recognize as the hidden item if stumbled upon.) Flashlight scavenger hunts begin as an extremely easy step. Just going into the dark room, without the door closed for 20 seconds evoked a full blown panic attack in my child. This took about 20 minutes to accomplish this the first few days. It took about a week of an easy hiding spot with the door open until we were able to begin to make it slightly harder. After about 2 weeks, we were able to close the door for her to look for the items.

This technique was key for her to accept the silence and the darkness as normal and for her to be comfortable in the same environment at nighttime. It worked amazingly well! As time progressed, items were hidden harder and harder so she really had to spend some significant time searching which, in turn, allowed her to spend more and more time in the dark. The idea of providing stickers, candy, tickets used for reward chart, or small prizes also can be used to evoke more excitement about searching for the reward. We also used this technique to decrease her fear of going to other areas of our home alone such as the basement with success. We would provide her a chore to do downstairs such as placing something in storage or bringing an item from the freezer to allow her to focus on something else other than the darkness to desensitize her to the darkness and fearful items.

Bedtime Passes

Bedtime passess were referenced in the book to establish healthy boundaries as the bedtime routine is progressing. My daughter's physician recommended 2 bedtime passess. Following my daughter going into her room and her bed, she was allowed up to 2 bedtime passes, if needed, to come to my room for additional support. Ideally, these would not be needed, and the the child will remain in their bed. We all know this is not a foolproof plan and each child is different. My daughter was so excited to earn her points that she rarely used these. Once a child has been placed in bed, if needed, they may come down for extra support 2 times. Once they have used the 2 passes, they are not getting any points on the reward chart. This can allow for 2 points per day to be earned if passess are not utilized. Once the 2 passess had been "cashed in," the points are gone and, we would move on to the sleeping bag method of sleep distance.

Sleeping Bag Distance

From the first day you begin this program, I would recommend stopping all sleeping in the bed with you. The sleeping bag distance method allows the child to sleep in your room (initially), and the space gradually gets farther and farther progressing to the child's room. Alternately, some parents sleep in the child's bed for comfort. This can work in reverse and the parent can gradually move the distance they are to their bedroom. (Although, sleeping on the floor as a parent can be none too comfortable!).

After the second bedtime pass is used, the child is placed on the sleeping bag beside your bed. This establishes a clear area of comfort for the child but not in the bed with you. This sleeping bag area should not be left from night to night as this provides the expectation they will return there again the next night. The child will need to pick up their space in the morning and return it to their room. The sleeping area below or directly beside the bed can go on for a couple nights depending on how comfortable or uncomfortable the child is not being in bed with you. Every few nights, the sleeping bag area gets closer and closer the child's room. With my child, it eventually was more comfortable and secure for her to sleep in her own room as a result of the other interventions we had been working on, versus sleeping on the sleeping bag in the hall. She decided to just sleep in her own bed I was actually amazed how fast this process worked!

Quiet Time Activities

As mentioned in the children's book, no electronics are recommended at nighttime, especially if you can provide a dim light. Prior to bedtime, allow your child to be in their room doing a quiet activity such as reading, playing building blocks, playing with dolls, playing with cars, crafts, or cleaning the room. This will limit the bright light stimulation of screen time and allow the body to begin to be in nighttime mode.

Follow Through and Consistency

Trust me when I tell you follow through is the key to success. We have been working at this nearly a year. At times, we felt like she was "fixed", and we rewarded her with sleeping in our bed but, unfortunately, it is like many other addictions. If you fall off the wagon and revert back, the process starts over again. We had told ourselves she would be fine, and we wanted her to have security, but that process failed over and over. Now, we consistently say no. It is particularly challenging when she has nightmares. For ten years of her life we held her close to calm her down. Now, we use distraction techniques and although we may cuddle for a few minutes for security, we then return her to her own bed to avoid breaking the healthy routine we have established. Consistency, consistency, consistency… you must keep the rules the same. You must keep the expectations the same. You must keep the consequences the same. Consistency keeps the positive results the same.

Through much hard work on our part as parents and more importantly hard work on my child's part, she now has a healthy bedtime routine. I now sleep through the night, and finally I also feel like I am getting a restful sleep in addition to my child. This is so important for me to be there for my family, my patients and myself. I pray that you and your child will find some helpful strategies in this book and find some peace in the chaos of life. As I negotiate life and continue with children and patients with anxiety, it is a learning process each day. I hope to inspire you and your family to begin a new routine and change your life the way our life has been changed over the last year. As we continue on this path, we will be publishing additional books in the series. I hope that you and your child enjoy reading them and working through the strategies. I hope that you enjoy reading as much as we have enjoyed creating the character and writing this book!

“Cast all your anxiety on Him because he cares for you”
(New International Version, 1 Peter 5:7)

“When you lie down, you will not be afraid, when you lie down, your sleep will be sweet.”
(Proverbs 3:24 NIV)

“Do not be anxious about anything, but in every situation, by prayer and petition, with thanksgiving, present your requests to God. And the peace of God, which transcends all understanding, will guard your hearts and your minds in Christ Jesus. “
(Philippians 4:6-7 NIV)

“The Lord gives strength to his people; the Lord blesses his people with peace”
(Psalm 29:11NIV)

“In peace I will both lie down and sleep; for you alone, O Lord, make me dwell in safety
(Psalm 4:8 NIV)

“Come to me, all you who are weary and burdened, and I will give you rest. Take my yoke upon you and learn from me, for I am gentle and humble in heart, and you will find rest for you souls.
For my yoke is easy and my burden is light.”
(Matthew 11:28-30 NIV)

There is no fear in love. But perfect love drives out fear, because fear has to do with punishment.
The one who fears is not made perfect in love.
(1 John 4:18 NIV)

Bibliography

New International Version. [Colorado Springs]: Biblica, 2011. BibleGateway.com. Web. 3 Mar. 2011.

97119697R00024

Made in the USA
San Bernardino, CA
21 November 2018